Sherlock Holmes and Dr Watson's Disappearance

Mabel Swift

Sherlock Holmes and Dr Watson's Disappearance

(A Sherlock Holmes Mystery - Book 10)

By

Mabel Swift

Copyright 2025 by Mabel Swift

www.mabelswift.com

All rights reserved. No part of this publication may be reproduced in any form, electronically or mechanically without permission from the author.

This is a work of fiction and any resemblance to any person living or dead is purely coincidental.

Contents

Chapter 1	1
Chapter 2	8
Chapter 3	18
Chapter 4	21
Chapter 5	27
Chapter 6	35
Chapter 7	44
Chapter 8	53
Chapter 9	62
Chapter 10	68
Chapter 11	75
Chapter 12	83
Chapter 13	92
Chapter 14	102

| Chapter 15 | 111 |
| A note from the author | 116 |

Chapter 1

Sherlock Holmes sat alone at the breakfast table inside 221B Baker Street. He glanced at the clock on the mantelpiece for the third time that morning. It was almost ten o'clock. Dr Watson was never late for breakfast, yet his chair remained conspicuously vacant. Most unusual.

Mrs Hudson entered with a pot of tea.

Holmes asked, "Mrs Hudson, do you know what has happened to Dr Watson this morning?"

"He received a telegram just before seven. I heard the messenger at the door, but Dr Watson got there before I did." Mrs Hudson poured tea into Holmes' cup. "He hurried back to his room and then came back downstairs in quite a rush with his medical bag. He said there was an urgent case requiring his attention."

"Did he mention where he was going?"

"Rose Lane, in Clerkenwell. He didn't give me the number of the house he was visiting. He assured me he would return home straight afterwards." Mrs Hudson frowned. "That was nearly three hours ago now."

Holmes said, "Was the telegram left behind? Perhaps with the patient's details?"

"None that I saw, Mr Holmes."

By twelve o'clock, Holmes had grown decidedly uneasy. He quickly searched Watson's room in case the telegram had been left there, but he didn't find anything.

Another hour passed and there was still no sign of Watson.

Holmes donned his coat and hat. He found Mrs Hudson in the kitchen and said to her, "I'm concerned about Dr Watson's absence. I shall make inquiries in Clerkenwell and see what I can discover."

Mrs Hudson nodded. "Will you let me know what you find out, please? I'm concerned about him, too."

Holmes said he would. He left the building and hailed a hansom cab.

"Clerkenwell," he instructed the driver as he climbed in. "Rose Lane."

A while later, the cab deposited Holmes at the entrance to Rose Lane. It was a narrow street with modest dwellings.

Holmes knocked at the first door. A young woman answered, but said she hadn't summoned a doctor that morning. Neither had the next household, nor the one after that. House by house, Holmes made his way down Rose Lane, each inquiry yielding the same result: no one had called for medical assistance.

At the final house, number thirty-three, an elderly woman answered his knock.

"A doctor? Why yes, a gentleman did call this morning. Said he was Dr Watson and that he was expected to attend to a child with fever."

Holmes asked, "What time was this?"

"About half past seven, I should think. Maybe a bit later. I had to tell him he was mistaken. No children live here, only myself. He seemed most puzzled by it. He checked a piece of paper in his pocket twice."

"Did you observe where he went afterwards?"

"I did. I watched him walk away. He stood at the end of the street looking confused. And then a cab pulled up next to him. A young woman leaned out and called out something to him."

"Did you hear what she said?"

"No, I didn't. My hearing isn't what it once was. The doctor approached the cab, spoke to the woman and looked like he was going to climb inside. That's the last I saw before closing my door."

Holmes thanked the woman and walked to the end of the street. He scanned the cobblestones and the surrounding area. Something caught his eye.

A small leather-bound book lay partly concealed in the gutter. Holmes picked it up, his face grave as he recognised Watson's precious journal. Watson would never discard it so carelessly.

He examined the street more carefully and noticed several fresh scratches on the cobblestones where a carriage had departed in haste.

His suspicions crystallised into certainty. Watson had not gone willingly. The telegram, the supposed medical emergency, was an elaborate ruse. Watson may not have gone willingly into the cab. Holmes suspected he had dropped his journal on purpose to leave a clue for him.

But who had taken Watson? And for what purpose?

Holmes tucked the journal into his coat pocket. He hastened away from Rose Lane and to a busier street where he caught the first available cab.

"Scotland Yard," he instructed the driver.

Holmes soon arrived at Scotland Yard and went inside. The building bustled with frantic activity. Constables rushed back and forth carrying stacks of papers, while clerks shouted across the room. A group of bedraggled men huddled in a corner no doubt awaiting processing for whatever crimes they had committed.

Holmes navigated through the chaos, dodging harried officers until he reached Inspector Lestrade's office. The inspector was buried behind towering piles of case files, looking thoroughly exhausted.

"I require your assistance," Holmes said without knocking.

Lestrade glanced up, dark circles beneath his eyes. "Mr Holmes. As you can see, we're rather occupied today." He gestured to the mountains of paperwork. "Three robberies in Mayfair, a suspicious fire in Whitechapel, and a murdered businessman in Kensington."

"Dr Watson has disappeared. He was lured away by a false medical emergency, and I believe, intercepted in Clerkenwell this morning."

Lestrade sighed, rubbing his forehead. "Are you certain? Dr Watson has many patients. Perhaps he's simply attending to one or more of them and has lost track of time."

Holmes placed Watson's journal on the desk. "He was last seen approaching a cab at the end of Rose Lane. This was around half past seven, perhaps a little later. He left this behind. He would never part with this willingly which suggests he has been taken against his will. He was supposed to return to Baker Street hours ago. Something is amiss here, Inspector."

"Mr Holmes, we're inundated with crimes requiring immediate attention. The doctor may have dropped that journal by accident. He has only been missing since this morning. He may well turn up later today with a perfectly reasonable explanation."

Holmes' expression hardened. "I don't think that will be the case. Tell me if you would, has there been an increase in kidnappings lately?"

Lestrade hesitated, then nodded reluctantly. "Yes, as a matter of fact. We've had a few more notifications of such crimes lately, and my officers are dealing with them. The criminals who are behind these incidents are dangerous people. I strongly advise you not to go looking for them, if that's your plan. If Dr Watson doesn't turn up by the end of the day, come back here and we'll handle this through proper channels."

Holmes said nothing, his face betraying no emotion as he retrieved Watson's journal from the desk. Without another word, he turned and departed, leaving Lestrade calling after him to no avail.

Holmes caught a cab and was taken away from Scotland Yard. Was Watson being held somewhere and possibly against his will? Holmes would find him, no matter what action he had to take even if that meant risking his own safety.

Chapter 2

Holmes stopped at The Blindman's Rest, a smoke-filled tavern frequented by those who existed between lawful society and outright criminality. The establishment reeked of stale beer and tobacco, and the floorboards were sticky beneath his boots. The din of raucous conversation diminished slightly as he entered, several patrons glancing up with wary recognition before returning to their drinks.

In a dimly lit corner sat Barker, a former pugilist with a mangled ear and a scar that bisected his left eyebrow. His broad hands, once powerful enough to fell men in the boxing ring, now curled around a glass of gin. He nodded almost imperceptibly as Holmes approached.

"Mr Holmes," Barker said. "To what do I owe this pleasure?"

Holmes slid onto the bench opposite him. "I require information about a matter of some delicacy."

"Information costs, as you well know." Barker took a sip of his drink.

Holmes placed several coins on the table. "I am investigating a kidnapping. A respected client of mine received a telegram early this morning, summoning him to Rose Lane in Clerkenwell on an urgent matter. When he arrived, he discovered the summons was false. He was last seen approaching a cab with a woman inside; a woman who had called out to him."

Barker pocketed the coins. "Sounds like Garrison's work."

"Garrison?"

"Victor Garrison. He runs a gang that specialises in such matters. They've taken to kidnapping well-to-do gentlemen these past six months. Their method is always the same. A false message, a meeting in a quiet location, then they spirit away the target before anyone notices they are missing."

"What is their purpose?"

"Ransom, primarily," Barker replied. "They demand substantial sums for the safe return of their captives."

"Has anyone ever been harmed during these kidnappings?" Holmes asked, his face betraying nothing of his inner thoughts.

Barker's expression grew grave. "Two victims were returned with broken fingers. Another was found in the Thames last month. The official verdict was suicide, but those in my circle know better."

"I see." Holmes's voice remained calm, but his eyes hardened. "Where might I find this Garrison?"

Barker stared at him. "You cannot mean to confront him directly."

"I merely wish to eliminate him as a suspect."

"The man is dangerous. He employs brutes and cutthroats. If you value your continued good health, I strongly advise against such a course of action."

"Nevertheless, I must pursue every avenue of inquiry."

Barker sighed with resignation. "He operates from the old Cooper's warehouse on Jacob Street. But I warn you, tread carefully. Garrison is not known for his tolerance of interference."

"I shall bear that in mind."

Holmes left The Blindman's Rest and stepped out into the bustling London street. A light mist had begun to fall, turning the cobblestones slick and causing passersby to hurry with collars turned up against the damp.

He hailed a cab, the driver hunched against the weather atop his perch.

"Jacob Street," Holmes instructed as he climbed inside, settling onto the worn leather seat.

The cab lurched into motion, joining the congested flow of vehicles. Through the window, Holmes observed London transforming as they travelled east and south. The respectable townhouses gave way to narrower buildings, the streets growing more confined and less maintained with every mile.

They crossed London Bridge. The Thames below was swollen and grey, dotted with barges and steamers.

The cab turned onto Jamaica Road, passing warehouses and wharves where dock workers unloaded cargo from around the world.

"This is as far as I go," the cabbie announced, pulling up at a corner. "Jacob Street is just ahead, but I've no business down there. It's a rough sort of place."

Holmes paid the man and stepped down onto the pavement. Suspicious faces watched from shadowed doorways. He proceeded onwards, his stride purposeful despite the unsavoury surroundings.

Cooper's warehouse loomed against the grey sky, its brick façade blackened with decades of London soot. Holmes noticed two men standing guard at the main entrance. They were dressed as labourers, but their stance and vigilance marked them clearly as sentries.

Holmes approached. The guards tensed as he drew near.

"State your business," the taller of the two demanded, one hand moving to his coat pocket.

"I wish to speak with Mr Garrison on a private matter," Holmes replied evenly.

The men exchanged glances. "And who might you be?"

"My name is Holmes. Sherlock Holmes."

The shorter guard's eyes widened slightly in recognition. "Wait here," he instructed, before disappearing inside the warehouse.

Holmes stood patiently, ignoring the remaining guard's suspicious stare. After several minutes, the man returned.

"This way," he grunted. "But I'm going to search you first."

Holmes submitted to a thorough pat-down, during which the guard removed a small pocket knife.

"You'll get this back when you leave," the man said, "assuming Mr Garrison permits you to leave." He indicated for Holmes to go inside.

The interior of the warehouse was cavernous, with high ceilings from which hung oil lamps that cast an uneven, yellowish light. The space had been divided into sections by wooden partitions. Several men lounged about, playing cards or cleaning weapons. They watched Holmes pass with undisguised hostility.

At the far end of the warehouse was a private office, its walls constructed of salvaged timber and glass panels. Inside, seated behind a substantial desk, was a tall man with a closely cropped beard and cold, calculating eyes. Despite the warmth of the building, he wore an immaculately tailored frock coat.

"Mr Sherlock Holmes," he said, his voice surprisingly cultured. "This is indeed unexpected. I am Victor Garrison."

Garrison gestured to a chair across from his desk. "Please, be seated. I confess I am curious about what brings London's most celebrated detective to my humble establishment."

Holmes remained standing. "I prefer to stand, thank you."

"As you wish." Garrison's smile did not reach his eyes. "Though I should warn you, my men find it disrespectful when guests refuse my hospitality."

Holmes glanced around, noting that three burly men had positioned themselves behind him, effectively blocking the exit.

"I would hate to offend," Holmes said, lowering himself into the chair.

"Much better. Now, to what do I owe this visit? I doubt you are here to request my services."

"I am investigating the disappearance of a gentleman," Holmes stated. "He was lured to Rose Lane this morning under false pretences and subsequently vanished."

Garrison's expression remained impassive. "And you suspect my involvement in this matter?"

"I am exploring all possibilities."

"I see." Garrison leaned back in his chair. "And the name of this businessman?"

"I prefer not to say."

Garrison laughed. "Discretion, even here? Very well. But I fail to see how I can assist you if you withhold such pertinent details."

"The method of abduction bears similarities to operations attributed to your organisation. Or so I've been told."

A flash of anger crossed Garrison's face. "You come into my domain and accuse me of kidnapping?"

"I make no accusations," Holmes replied calmly. "I merely seek information."

One of the men behind Holmes stepped forward, but Garrison raised a hand, halting him.

"You are either very brave or very foolish, Mr Holmes," Garrison said "Men have disappeared for less impertinence."

"I am intent on finding the missing gentleman," Holmes said. "I have no wish to offend you."

The tension in the room was palpable. One of the men behind Holmes cracked his knuckles loudly.

Garrison studied Holmes for a long moment, then unexpectedly smiled. "You have courage, I grant you that. But as it happens, I can assure you that my organisation is not responsible for the disappearance of your client."

"You seem quite certain."

"I am. We have been otherwise engaged this past fortnight with a separate venture."

Holmes raised an eyebrow. "I see. If not your organisation, then who?"

Garrison shrugged. "London harbours many desperate men capable of extreme actions. Perhaps your businessman has rivals? Or colleagues who resent him for some reason, someone with cause to wish him harm? Perhaps he is involved in matters more sordid than you realise."

Holmes stood. "I thank you for your time, Mr Garrison."

"A moment, Mr Holmes." Garrison rose from his desk, towering over Holmes by several inches. "I have answered your questions. In return, I would ask that my name does not feature in any future discussions you might have with the police."

"I am not in the habit of making promises I may be unable to keep."

Garrison continued, "Then let me be clear. Should my operations face increased scrutiny as a result of your visit, I shall be most displeased. And you would not wish to displease me, Mr Holmes."

"Are you threatening me, Mr Garrison?"

"Merely stating facts." Garrison smiled thinly. "Simpson will show you out."

A guard stepped forward, gesturing towards the door.

As Holmes turned to leave, Garrison spoke again. "I hope you find your businessman, Mr Holmes. London can be such a dangerous city for the unwary."

Holmes departed the warehouse, his expression betraying nothing of his thoughts. The guard returned his pocket knife.

Holmes strode away from the warehouse, his mind racing with possibilities. Had Watson been abducted for more personal reasons like Garrison had suggested? Something to do with his profession perhaps?

The answer, he suspected, lay either in Watson's past or in their shared history of cases. Of course, there was the possibility that someone had taken Watson as an act of revenge against Holmes. But he would deal with that as a possibility later once he had looked into Watson's past.

Chapter 3

Holmes returned to Baker Street, his mind occupied with the troubling circumstances of Watson's disappearance.

Mrs Hudson greeted him at the door, her face drawn with concern. "Any news of Dr Watson, Mr Holmes?"

"Not as yet," Holmes replied, removing his hat and coat.

"It's not like him to vanish without a proper word," she said. "He's always been so considerate. I fear something dreadful has happened."

Holmes regarded the landlady's anxious expression and decided against sharing his suspicions.

"I'm sure I'll locate him soon. Tell me, would you happen to know where Watson keeps journals about his medical career? Perhaps those dating back to his training days."

"I do," Mrs Hudson replied. "But why do you ask? Oh, Mr Holmes, do you think his disappearance has something to do with his medical work?"

"Please don't trouble yourself unduly," Holmes said with a reassuring gesture. "It's merely a line of inquiry I wish to explore. Where might these journals be found?"

"In his room. On the bookshelf beside his writing desk. The medical journals are properly dated and organised. Dr Watson is most particular about his records."

Holmes nodded. "Thank you, Mrs Hudson. Perhaps you might prepare some tea while I look through them?"

After the landlady departed for the kitchen, Holmes climbed the stairs to Watson's bedroom. The room was neat and orderly, reflecting its occupant's military background. True to Mrs Hudson's word, a row of journals stood on the bookshelf, each bearing a year inscribed in gold lettering on the spine.

Holmes pulled them out one by one, arranging them chronologically on Watson's desk. The collection spanned from his early medical training through his military service in Afghanistan and into his current practice. It would take considerable time to review them all, but Holmes was determined to do so.

"What secrets do you hold, old friend?" Holmes murmured, opening the earliest volume.

He began his methodical search, looking for any record of complaints or disagreements from fellow doctors or any other professionals he may have worked with over the years.

The first several journals yielded nothing of note. Watson's early career had been unremarkable, filled with the typical challenges of a medical student and young doctor. His military service records were more harrowing but revealed no obvious enemies.

Holmes carefully documented each potential lead, but none seemed substantial enough to explain Watson's abduction. He continued his examination of the journals, determined to find the answer.

Finally, he spotted an entry which greatly troubled him.

Chapter 4

Holmes studied the journal entry. It concerned a Dr Nathaniel Wicklow. Twenty years prior, Watson had served briefly as Dr Wicklow's assistant during his rounds. Later, Watson had been called as an expert witness in a legal case against the surgeon.

According to Watson's meticulous notes, he had testified regarding improper surgical procedures employed by Wicklow that had resulted in the death of a wealthy aristocrat's son. Watson's testimony, delivered with characteristic honesty, had contributed significantly to the ruling against the surgeon. Though Wicklow had avoided criminal charges, his professional standing had suffered considerably, resulting in the loss of numerous lucrative clients.

The final entry regarding Wicklow noted the surgeon's barely concealed anger as he left the courtroom. Watson had written: "I fear I have made an enemy today, though I could not in good conscience have testified otherwise."

Had Wicklow been harbouring a grudge against Watson after all these years? And if so, what might have happened recently to provoke him into possible action? Holmes considered the timeline carefully. The abduction had been meticulously planned, requiring knowledge of Watson's habits and character. Such planning suggested a deeply personal motive.

He rose from the chair, placing the journal carefully back with the others. The evidence, though circumstantial, warranted further investigation. A visit to Dr Wicklow seemed the most logical course of action.

Holmes consulted the medical directory on Watson's shelf, quickly locating Wicklow's entry. The surgeon now maintained a private practice in Harley Street and also worked as a surgeon at St Thomas' Hospital. The directory noted his prestigious appointments and specialisations, suggesting Wicklow had successfully rebuilt his reputation in the years since the scandal.

Holmes decided to try Harley Street first and set off without delay.

A while later, he arrived at Dr Wicklow's practice which occupied an elegant building with large windows and an imposing front door. The brass plate beside the entrance gleamed in the afternoon light, bearing the surgeon's name and credentials in ornate lettering. Holmes was admitted by a well-dressed attendant who led him through to a waiting room furnished with expensive chairs and adorned with paintings of rural landscapes.

After a brief wait, Holmes was shown into Wicklow's private consultation room, where the surgeon greeted him cordially.

"Mr Sherlock Holmes," said Wicklow, offering his hand. "Please, do sit down."

Holmes took the offered seat, observing the surgeon closely. Wicklow was a tall man with an aristocratic bearing. His hands were smooth and well-maintained, the hands of a man who took great pride in his surgical skill.

"I imagine you are wondering why I have called upon you, Dr Wicklow," Holmes began.

"Indeed I am. How may I be of service to you, Mr Holmes?"

"I am here concerning Dr John Watson," Holmes said. "He has gone missing under troubling circumstances."

Holmes watched Wicklow's face intently, searching for any flicker of recognition or guilt. The surgeon's expression remained composed.

"Missing? That is most concerning. When did this occur?"

"This morning. He received what appears to have been a false summons to attend a patient in Clerkenwell. He has not been seen since."

"And you suspect my involvement?" Wicklow asked, raising an eyebrow.

"I am exploring all possibilities," Holmes replied evenly. "In reviewing Dr Watson's journals, I discovered a record of an incident twenty years ago involving yourself. He served as an expert witness in a case that damaged your professional standing considerably."

Wicklow's expression softened, and to Holmes' surprise, he smiled slightly.

"Ah, yes. The Belford case. It was indeed a difficult time. Dr Watson's testimony was damaging, certainly, but it was also honest. While I admit that at the time I felt considerable bitterness towards Dr Watson, twenty years is a long time to nurse a grievance."

"Nevertheless, resentments can lie dormant for years before circumstances revive them," Holmes countered. "I wonder, has anything occurred recently that might have rekindled old animosities between you and Dr Watson?"

"Nothing whatsoever," Wicklow replied. "In fact, I encountered Dr Watson at a medical conference last month, and we spoke briefly but pleasantly. There was no tension between us."

"What was the nature of this conversation?" Holmes asked.

Wicklow replied, "Professional matters only. An interesting case of septicaemia that had been presented that morning. Watson expressed some fascinating theories regarding prevention."

Holmes studied Wicklow's face for any sign of deception but found his expression difficult to read. "I must ask, where were you this morning between seven and eight o'clock?"

"A fair question. I was performing an urgent surgery at St Thomas' Hospital from half past six until nearly eleven. There were two assisting surgeons present, three nurses, and an observing medical student. You are welcome to verify this with the hospital administration."

Holmes said he would do that and asked for the relevant details of the witnesses. He then continued, "Do you know of anyone who might wish Dr Watson harm? Perhaps someone connected to your circle who might have taken offence on your behalf?"

Wicklow considered this for a moment. "None that come to mind. Dr Watson is generally well-regarded in medical circles, despite that old business with me. I cannot imagine anyone harbouring genuine ill will towards him."

Holmes rose from his chair. "Thank you for your time, Dr Wicklow."

"I hope you find Dr Watson promptly and safely, Mr Holmes," Wicklow said, standing as well. "Despite our professional differences, I have always respected his dedication to truth. If I can be of any further assistance, please do not hesitate to call upon me."

Holmes departed Wicklow's practice and stopped on the pavement outside to consider his next move. Somewhere in London, Watson was possibly being held against his will. Holmes felt a tightening in his chest at the thought of his friend in danger; his friend who had stood by him through countless perils without complaint.

If Wicklow was not responsible for Watson's disappearance, then who was? The false summons to Clerkenwell suggested someone who knew Watson would respond immediately to a medical emergency.

Holmes needed to investigate further.

Chapter 5

After paying a visit to St Thomas' Hospital to confirm Wicklow's alibi, Holmes arrived back at Baker Street. He removed his coat and hat, hanging them carefully before making his way upstairs to the sitting room. The familiar surroundings of their lodgings provided little comfort given Watson's continued absence. He sank into his armchair.

A few minutes later, Mrs Hudson entered carrying a tray.

"Any word about Dr Watson?" Holmes asked her.

"Nothing at all, Mr Holmes," she replied, setting down a pot of tea and a plate of sandwiches on a side table. "I've kept watch at the window all afternoon, hoping Dr Watson might return." She poured him a cup of tea. "Have you discovered anything?"

Holmes studied the landlady's worried expression. Holmes realised he could no longer protect her from the truth. Moreover, he might need her assistance.

"Mrs Hudson," Holmes said, accepting the cup she offered, "I believe the time has come to speak plainly. Dr Watson has not simply been delayed by a medical emergency."

Mrs Hudson sighed heavily. "I feared as much. What has happened to him?"

Holmes gestured for her to sit. "I have reason to believe he has been abducted. The telegram he received this morning was a carefully constructed ruse to lure him away. When he arrived in Clerkenwell, someone intercepted him and took him away by cab, possibly against his will."

Mrs Hudson's hand flew to her mouth, but she remained composed. "Oh, poor Dr Watson. Who would do such a terrible thing?"

"That is what I am attempting to determine," Holmes said. "I have looked through Dr Watson's journals for any disputes he may have had with colleagues or other professionals. I followed a lead to a man called Dr Wicklow, whom Watson testified against years ago, but I have checked his alibi and it appears sound."

"Surely Scotland Yard can help?" Mrs Hudson asked hopefully.

Holmes set down his cup. "Inspector Lestrade believes it's too early to mount an official search. He suggested we wait until the end of the day."

"But that could be too late!" Mrs Hudson exclaimed, her normally composed demeanour faltering.

"My thoughts precisely," Holmes said. "I've examined Watson's journals, but perhaps I've been looking for the wrong pattern. Not someone with a grudge against Watson professionally, but someone with an unhealthy fixation."

Mrs Hudson considered this. "You mean one of his patients?"

"Precisely. Watson once mentioned that certain patients become unduly attached to their physicians. Those with imagined ailments can be particularly demanding of a doctor's time and attention."

"A hypochondriac, you mean?" Mrs Hudson asked.

"Exactly so," Holmes replied. "Consider this scenario: Watson attends to a patient repeatedly but finds no genuine medical complaint. Eventually, he must withdraw his services. The patient, distressed by this perceived abandonment, takes desperate measures to ensure Watson remains within their reach."

Mrs Hudson's eyes widened. "By kidnapping him? That sounds like madness, Mr Holmes."

"To rational minds, perhaps," Holmes agreed. "But to someone consumed by anxiety and fixation, it might seem perfectly logical."

"I never thought of it that way," Mrs Hudson admitted. "Can I do something to help, Mr Holmes? Anything at all?"

"I need to examine Watson's medical records again," Holmes said. "Your help with that would be greatly appreciated. We should look for patients he saw frequently without providing significant treatment. A pattern of visits with no conclusive diagnosis."

Mrs Hudson nodded firmly. "Shall we make a start now?"

They gathered the journals and brought them into the sitting room. Dividing them between them, Holmes and Mrs Hudson began their search with the most recent journals.

The room fell silent save for the occasional rustle of pages and the ticking of the mantel clock, each second marking Watson's lengthening absence.

"Most entries are quite brief," Mrs Hudson observed after twenty minutes of careful reading. "'Mrs Thompson, bronchitis, prescribed bed rest and tincture.' 'Mr Barrow, sprained ankle, applied bandage.' How shall we determine which patients might have been troublesome?"

Holmes looked up from the journal he was examining. "Watson is methodical. He would have noted difficult cases in some consistent manner. Look for repeated visits to the same patient, or perhaps some annotation to indicate his frustration."

They continued their search.

"Mr Holmes," Mrs Hudson said suddenly. "I believe I've found something. Dr Watson has marked certain entries with a small asterisk."

Holmes raised his eyebrows. "An asterisk? Show me."

He moved to look over her shoulder. There, beside an entry for a Lady Hartley complaining of unexplained fatigue, was indeed a small asterisk inked in Watson's neat hand.

"Excellent observation, Mrs Hudson. I must admit, I hadn't noticed such markings during my previous search," Holmes said. He shook his head. "But I should have noticed them. This could be Dr Watson's system for highlighting problematic cases and I completely missed it. I have wasted valuable time!"

Mrs Hudson said, "Don't be so hard on yourself. Dr Watson is your friend, and you are concerned about him."

"Even so, I let my emotions get in the way of my observations. That won't happen again. Now, let us look further at these markings."

With this new understanding, they redoubled their efforts, searching specifically for the telling symbol among Watson's careful records.

"Here's another for the same patient," Mrs Hudson noted, turning pages. "And again three days later. 'Lady Hartley, complaints of heart palpitations, no physical cause found.' Dr Watson has marked it with an asterisk again."

"The pattern is becoming clearer," Holmes said. "Ah, here's a different patient with similar annotations. 'Mr Penrose, claims of mysterious numbness in extremities, no clinical evidence observed.' Also marked with an asterisk."

They continued their methodical search, finding occasional asterisked entries scattered throughout Watson's records. But it was Mrs Hudson who made the crucial discovery.

"Mr Holmes," she said, her voice suddenly tense with excitement. "I believe I've found something significant."

She placed a journal before him, open to the latest entry that was dated three days ago. "The Duchess of Bellington. Look at how many times she appears in just the past two months."

Holmes examined the pages carefully. The Duchess had summoned Watson seventeen times over the last two months, each visit featuring a new complaint: chest pains, difficulty breathing, mysterious aches, sudden weakness. Yet Watson's notes consistently indicated he could find no medical explanation for any of her symptoms.

Watson's final entry, dated just three days ago, was particularly revealing: 'I can find no physical cause for Her Grace's complaints. I suspect her ailments are of a nervous disposition, possibly stemming from profound loneliness since her husband's passing last year. I must gently but firmly explain that I can be of no further medical assistance and recommend she consult a specialist in nervous disorders. I shall send her a letter immediately.'

The entry was marked with not one but two asterisks.

"This is most promising," Holmes said. "The Duchess repeatedly sought Watson's attention for complaints he could neither verify nor treat. And now he has disappeared, immediately after deciding to withdraw his services."

"You think she's keeping him captive?" Mrs Hudson asked.

Holmes replied, "The Duchess of Bellington may be someone who is accustomed to wielding considerable influence. If Watson attempted to remove himself from her service, she might have taken measures to ensure he couldn't leave her. Perhaps she paid someone to arrange for this to happen."

"Would she really do such a thing?" Mrs Hudson asked.

"I intend to find out. I must visit her immediately. Where does the Duchess reside?"

Mrs Hudson consulted the journal once more. "According to this, she maintains a townhouse in Mayfair, on Berkeley Square."

Holmes said, "I will go there now. If Watson returns while I'm gone, or if any message arrives from him, send word to me there at once."

"Do be careful," Mrs Hudson cautioned. "If this woman is truly capable of arranging Dr Watson's abduction, there is no telling what other actions she might take."

"I shall exercise every caution," Holmes assured her. "But I cannot delay. Every hour increases the danger to Watson."

With that, he left the dwelling and headed out into the street.

Chapter 6

Later, Holmes stood at the entrance of Berkeley Square, gazing at the imposing townhouse of the Duchess of Bellington. The late afternoon sky was beginning to darken over London. As he approached the residence, he carefully considered his strategy. Revealing Watson's disappearance to the Duchess might prove counterproductive if she was indeed involved. Better to approach indirectly and observe her reactions.

A butler, impeccably attired in formal livery, answered the door. Holmes presented his card.

"Mr Sherlock Holmes to see Her Grace," he stated calmly.

The butler examined the card with a raised eyebrow. "Does Her Grace expect you, sir?"

"No, but I believe she will wish to receive me. I come on behalf of Dr Watson."

At the mention of Watson's name, the butler's expression shifted slightly. "Please wait in the entrance hall, sir. I shall inquire if Her Grace is receiving visitors."

Holmes was left standing in a grand entrance hall adorned with ancestral portraits and elaborately framed landscapes. The floors were polished marble, and a crystal chandelier hung from the ceiling.

The butler returned after several minutes. "Her Grace will see you. Please follow me."

Holmes was led through a corridor lined with more family portraits to a spacious drawing room where the Duchess of Bellington reclined upon a sofa upholstered in burgundy velvet. A silver tray beside her held an impressive array of medicine bottles, tinctures, and tonics. Her pale hand rested against her forehead in what Holmes immediately recognised as a theatrical gesture of suffering.

"Mr Sherlock Holmes to see Your Grace," announced the butler, stepping aside to permit Holmes entrance.

"Thank you, Taylor. That will be all for now," the Duchess said, dismissing the butler with a languid wave.

Holmes bowed slightly. "Your Grace, I appreciate you receiving me without prior notice."

The Duchess regarded him with tired eyes. "Mr Holmes, the detective. What an unexpected visitor. Has something dreadful happened?"

"Not at all, Your Grace," Holmes replied smoothly. "I come on behalf of Dr Watson. He expressed concern about how you might have received his recent letter."

"Did he indeed?" The Duchess adjusted her position with exaggerated care. "How considerate of him to send his friend to soften the blow. I suppose he could not face me after abruptly terminating our professional relationship."

Holmes noted the bitterness in her tone. "Dr Watson felt it was in your best interest to consult a specialist in nervous disorders. He holds your health in the highest regard."

"My health?" The Duchess gave a brittle laugh. "My dear Mr Holmes, if Dr Watson truly cared for my health, he would not have abandoned me to suffer alone. I have been at death's door these past three months. My nerves are utterly shattered. I experience palpitations, shortness of breath, and such pain that some mornings I cannot rise from my bed."

"Most distressing," Holmes said.

"Dr Watson prescribed these pills." She indicated a small blue bottle with evident distaste. "They do nothing for my condition. Nothing at all."

"I am sorry to hear that. Dr Watson speaks highly of your fortitude in the face of such suffering."

This compliment softened her expression momentarily. "Does he? Well, perhaps he is not entirely without perception."

"He mentioned your case requires particular attention that he regrettably cannot provide."

"As it should," she declared, warming to the subject. "My symptoms confound ordinary medical knowledge. Last Tuesday, I experienced such a spasm in my left side that Taylor was forced to summon help. Dr Watson arrived, prescribed more of these useless pills, and suggested light exercise." She pronounced the latter as though he had recommended she undertake manual labour.

Holmes nodded sympathetically. "Medical science advances daily, yet some conditions remain mysterious."

The Duchess lowered her voice conspiratorially. "Between ourselves, Mr Holmes, I wonder if your friend is truly qualified for his position."

"Dr Watson's credentials are impeccable," Holmes replied mildly.

"Perhaps, but there are rumours."

Holmes' expression remained neutral. "Rumours?"

The Duchess seemed pleased to have captured his interest. "You haven't heard? I'm surprised, given your profession. My dear friend Mrs Hazel Redford used to tell me the most shocking things. She said Dr Watson was involved in something quite terrible. Something he covered up most carefully."

"I find that difficult to believe."

"All men have secrets." The Duchess adjusted her shawl about her shoulders. "Even your esteemed colleague. Though I did give him the benefit of the doubt when I employed his services."

"What precisely have you heard?"

"It concerns a death that Dr Watson was responsible for a suspicious death." The Duchess closed her eyes. "But I am suddenly overcome with fatigue. My condition, you understand. Perhaps you might call another day when I am stronger."

Holmes recognised the interview was at an end. "Of course, Your Grace. Thank you for your time."

She waved a languid hand in dismissal. "Taylor will show you out."

The butler materialised at Holmes' side, guiding him toward the entrance hall. As they walked through the corridor towards the entrance, Holmes addressed the butler.

"Taylor, might I ask how often Dr Watson visited Her Grace?"

"Three times last week alone, sir," Taylor replied stiffly. "Dr Watson has been remarkably patient with the Duchess. Far more accommodating than most physicians who have attended her."

"Her Grace mentioned rumours concerning Dr Watson and someone named Mrs Hazel Redford," Holmes said casually.

The butler's professional composure faltered momentarily. "Mrs Redford is a longstanding friend of the Duchess. I would not wish to speak ill of any associate of Her Grace's."

"Yet you seem troubled by the mention of her name," Holmes observed.

The butler hesitated. "It is not my place to comment, sir, but Mrs Redford has been known to make rather serious allegations about Dr Watson. On more than one occasion, I overheard her telling the Duchess that Dr Watson got away with murder and that justice will be done one day.

Most unsettling talk, though I pay little attention to such matters."

"Do you know where I might find Mrs Redford now?"

"I regret I cannot assist you in that regard, sir," Taylor replied. "Mrs Redford hasn't visited for years. I don't even know if Her Grace maintains any correspondence with her."

They reached the front door. Holmes thanked the butler and left the residence.

Holmes walked away, deep in thought. The surname Redford was familiar. He had seen it in Watson's journals, but he couldn't recall the details, which was incredibly frustrating.

He walked on, letting his mind grow clearer.

Mrs Hazel Redford. Why was her name familiar?

He walked some more.

The name Dr Harold Redford suddenly came to him

Holmes continued walking, letting his mind focus on Dr Redford and why that name was important.

After a few moments, he abruptly stopped walking and smiled. That was it.

He had seen the name in Watson's medical journals. He recalled the details clearly.

Dr Harold Redford had consulted Watson regarding a persistent and troubling illness. Watson had documented the progression of Redford's symptoms with his customary thoroughness. The initial complaints seemed ordinary enough: fatigue, weight loss, occasional digestive distress. But as the weeks passed, Redford's condition deteriorated markedly, and eventually crippling weakness confined him to his bed.

Watson's notes revealed his growing concern and frustration, and how his patient responded to treatment but then had relapsed into a worse state than before.

The final entries were particularly poignant. Watson had visited Redford daily during his last week, adjusting treatments and providing what comfort he could. He'd stated how Mrs Redford had remained admirably strong and that she had expressed sincere gratitude for Watson's efforts despite his inability to reverse her husband's decline.

Despite Watson doing all he could to heal Dr Redford, the man had passed away leaving behind his wife and a ten-year-old daughter called Sarah. Watson's final words were how he remained baffled by the nature of Redford's illness, and despite all medical interventions, his system simply failed. He added that Mrs Redford bore the news with dignity, thanking Watson for his attention.

So what had caused Mrs Redford to spread such malicious rumours about Watson?

Watson had noted the Redfords' address in his journal. It occurred to Holmes that Mrs Redford might still reside there. It was a tenuous possibility, but one worth investigating.

He would visit the Redford residence immediately. Though the hour was growing late, this could not wait until morning.

Chapter 7

Twenty minutes later, Holmes arrived at the residence where Dr Redford once lived. It was a grand townhouse with ornate iron railings and polished stone steps.

When Holmes knocked at the front door, it was opened by a housekeeper whose expression immediately soured upon seeing a visitor at such a late hour. She was a tall woman with hair pulled tightly back in a bun, her black dress impeccably pressed.

"Who are you? And what is your business?" she demanded.

"I apologise for the intrusion," Holmes said, removing his hat politely. He introduced himself and added, "I am seeking information about the Redford family. I've been told this is their family home, or at least, it was fifteen years ago."

The housekeeper's lips thinned with displeasure. "The Redfords? They don't live here anymore. I have been in service with the Claytons since they purchased this property about fourteen years ago."

"I see," Holmes replied. "May I ask if you might know where Mrs Redford relocated to?"

"You should return in the morning and speak with Mr Clayton. He might recall something from the purchase arrangements," she said, beginning to close the door.

Holmes placed his hand gently against the wood, preventing its closure. "Please, a man's life may depend on this information. Did Mrs Redford leave any forwarding address when she departed?"

The housekeeper hesitated, studying Holmes' face. Whatever she saw there must have convinced her of his sincerity, for her expression softened slightly.

"Wait here," she instructed.

She closed the door, leaving Holmes standing on the doorstep. He glanced at his pocket watch, acutely aware of each passing minute.

The door opened again. The housekeeper held a small notebook in her hands.

"When Mr Clayton purchased the house, Mrs Redford left her forwarding address in case any post should arrive for her here. It's twenty-seven Weavers Lane in Bethnal Green. Whether she remains there after all this time, I cannot say."

Holmes committed the address to memory. "Thank you. You have been most helpful."

Holmes nodded in farewell and then made his way to Bethnal Green.

The journey took him from the broad, tree-lined avenues of wealth to increasingly narrow streets where poverty pressed in from all sides.

Weavers Lane proved to be a modest terrace of brick houses, their exteriors weathered but largely respectable. Number twenty-seven stood in the middle of the row, its windows illuminated with the warm glow of lamp light.

Holmes rapped sharply on the door, which was opened by a stout woman in a plain grey dress and white apron. Her round face held the open, concerned expression of someone unaccustomed to receiving visitors after dark.

"I am looking for Mrs Redford or her daughter Sarah," Holmes announced without preamble.

The woman regarded him with cautious eyes. "Who is asking?"

"My name is Sherlock Holmes. It is a matter of some urgency."

Recognition flashed across the woman's face. "The detective? From the newspapers?"

"The same."

She invited him in and opened the door wider, allowing Holmes to step into a narrow hallway smelling of beeswax polish and fresh bread. "I'm the landlady here. Mrs Redford and her daughter, Sarah, are tenants of mine. They rent the upstairs rooms. Or rather, they were tenants. Mrs Redford passed away last month. Pneumonia took her quickly, poor soul."

"I'm sorry to hear that. And Miss Sarah Redford? Does she still live here"

"She does," the landlady confirmed. "Though she left me a note yesterday saying she was going away for a few days and didn't know when she would be back. It's most unlike her not to give me more notice. She has always been so considerate."

"Might I see her room?"

The landlady hesitated. "I am not in the habit of allowing strangers into my lodgers' private quarters."

"I understand your reluctance," Holmes said. "But it is a matter of considerable importance. I believe Miss Redford may have information vital to a case I am investigating."

The landlady studied his face for a moment, her expression uncertain.

"I assure you, madam, my intentions are honourable," Holmes added. "I merely wish to confirm whether Miss Redford has truly gone for just a few days as her note suggests."

"Well," the landlady hesitated, "I suppose there would be no harm in a quick look. Follow me, Mr Holmes."

She led him up a staircase to a door at the end of a corridor.

The room beyond was small but had been neatly kept. A single bed stood against one wall, a wardrobe against another. A writing desk occupied the space beneath the window, which overlooked a small courtyard below. Holmes swept his gaze across the room, noting the open, empty drawers of the bureau and the wardrobe door ajar revealing empty hangers.

Holmes said, "It appears Sarah Redford has taken all her belongings."

The landlady hovered in the doorway. "But her note said she would return in a few days."

"I fear that was not her true intention," Holmes replied.

His attention was caught by a crumpled newspaper protruding from beneath the bed. He retrieved it and smoothed it flat upon the desk. The front page bore an account of the most recent case he and Watson had solved together.

There, in the margin beside the detailed praise of Watson's crucial observations in the case, someone had drawn a vicious circle in black ink around Watson's name. Beneath it, a single word had been written: 'MURDERER!'

Holmes showed the newspaper to the landlady and asked, "What do you know about this?"

"Ah, Dr Watson," the landlady replied, clearly looking uncomfortable. "Sarah must have written that. Mrs Redford and Sarah had a very low opinion of Dr Watson."

"Why?" Holmes asked.

"Come downstairs, Mr Holmes. I shall make us some tea, and we can talk properly."

"I appreciate the offer, but time is of the essence," Holmes replied. "Please, tell me more about the Redfords' feelings about Dr Watson."

"Mrs Redford was the one who spoke harshly about Dr Watson. Usually after she'd had a glass of sherry in the evenings. She blamed Dr Watson for her husband's death. Sometimes she would say terrible things, that Dr Watson had deliberately allowed her husband to die, that he had robbed Sarah of her father. I never believed it myself. But what unsettled me most was that Mrs Redford said she would get revenge on Dr Watson one day, to hold him accountable for the death of her husband."

"Did Sarah share her mother's views?"

"She never contradicted them." The landlady sighed deeply. "I fear she'd been listening to them for so long, that she must have become of the same opinion regarding Dr Watson. Sarah was always a quiet girl, but when Mrs Redford passed last month, she became even more withdrawn. Barely spoke a word to anyone."

Holmes nodded. "Do you have any idea where Sarah may have gone? Did the Redfords have any other properties or relatives she might visit?"

"No relatives that I know of. Dr Redford was an only child, and Mrs Redford was estranged from her family after marrying beneath her station, as she once told me. They did speak of a cottage, though. Somewhere in Surrey, a village called Box Hill. They used to holiday there when Dr Redford was alive. Mrs Redford would reminisce about it sometimes. She said those were the happiest times of their lives. But they had to sell it after the doctor's death."

Holmes asked, "Do you recall anything specific about this cottage? Its location or appearance?"

"Only that it was quite isolated, surrounded by woodland. Mrs Redford mentioned how they would walk through the trees, and Dr Redford would point out the medicinal plants growing there." The landlady shook her head. "I am sorry I can't be more precise. Do you think Sarah may have gone there?"

"She may have. I shall make enquiries in Box Hill. Can I ask, do you know why Mrs Redford and her daughter took up lodgings with you? I have seen their former home and I wonder why Mrs Redford didn't stay there. And surely, the sale of the building would have allowed Mrs Redford to buy a house, albeit a more modest one."

The landlady replied, "Mrs Redford did confide in me one night about that. She said a friend of her husband's had sold the house for them because she was too grief-stricken to stay there without her husband, and emotionally she was not able to deal with such matters. This man advised her that the house hadn't been sold for what he was expecting, and in fact, it was a lot less. He gave the profits to Mrs Redford and her daughter and it allowed them to live much more modestly. I know Sarah was keen for them to live in their own house again one day and had put most of her wages into a savings account ever since she started working at a library about eight years ago."

"I wonder if she has taken those savings with her," Holmes mused. "This friend of Dr Redford's, do you know his name?"

"I don't, and I didn't think it was my business to pry."

"No, of course not," Holmes replied. "Thank you for your time. If Sarah returns here, would you let me know, please?" He handed her a card. "I will see myself out." He tipped his hat in farewell and hastened down the stairs.

Out on the street, Holmes calculated the fastest route to Surrey. It would take less than two hours by train and carriage, and with luck, he should locate the holiday home of the Redfords.

Would Sarah Redford be there? Had she been the woman who had forced Watson into the carriage earlier this morning? If so, had she worked alone or did she have an accomplice? Perhaps Garrison was involved in the kidnapping after all.

And what about Watson? Had Sarah Redford finally fulfilled her mother's fifteen-year wish for retribution against the doctor she blamed for her husband's death? Was Holmes already too late?

Chapter 8

A while later, Holmes sat alone in the first-class compartment of a train departing from Victoria Station. The carriage swayed gently as it gathered speed, carrying him away from London and towards Surrey, where he hoped to find Watson. He had taken the time to send a telegram to Mrs Hudson advising only that he was pursuing a new lead and would likely not return that evening. There was no point telling her not to worry because he was sure she would do that anyway.

Holmes considered the mind of Sarah Redford, who had lost her father at a young age; a patient whom Watson couldn't save. After listening to her mother's bitterness for years, she may have taken it upon herself to seek a terrible vengeance. Perhaps the death of her mother had been the catalyst, and seeing Watson's name in the newspaper was the spark that set her plan in motion. But what was Sarah

Redford capable of? How far would she go to avenge her father's death?

And, Holmes mused, who was this man who had sold the Redfords' house? This friend of the father's? The properties in that area were highly sought after. He didn't believe for a moment that the house sale had brought in a low amount. This man had lied to a recently bereaved mother. Was he connected to Watson's disappearance?

The rhythm of the train's wheels against the tracks marked the passing minutes. Holmes glanced repeatedly at his pocket watch, acutely aware that each second might be crucial for Watson. He found himself willing the train to move faster, though it was already travelling at a considerable speed. His usual calm demeanour was being tested by concern for his friend.

What seemed like an eternity later, the train stopped at Dorking station. Holmes disembarked and secured a cab to take him the remaining distance to Box Hill. The cabman, a weathered fellow with a greying beard, raised his eyebrows at the destination.

"Box Hill itself, sir? Not much up there this time of night but the darkness," he said, helping Holmes into the cab.

"I am looking for a cottage. One that belonged to the Redford family some years ago."

The cabman nodded slowly. "Ah, the old Redford place. It hasn't been lived in for years, that one. Gone to ruin, it has."

"You know of it?"

"Everyone around here knows of it. Nice little place it was, once. Doctor Redford and his family used to come down from London for holidays. That all stopped after he passed, poor fellow. It passed through a few new owners over the years, but it needed a lot of work done. And, well, I guess the repair costs were too high to tempt a new buyer. Are you interested in buying it?"

Holmes replied, "I am only interested in visiting it, and as soon as possible. Have you seen anything of Mrs Redford or her daughter since the passing of Dr Redford?"

"No, sir, I haven't." The cabman climbed into his seat, took the reins, and the horse set off at a brisk trot.

The road wound upward through woodland, the gradient becoming steeper as they climbed. The darkness of the night pressed in around them, the trees on either side of the narrow road occasionally illuminated by the cab's lamps. Holmes peered out at the shadowy landscape, every sense alert.

After a while, they reached a point where the road narrowed too much for the cab to continue.

"I'll have to let you down here, sir," the cabman said. "The cottage is about a quarter-mile further up, through those trees." He pointed to a narrow path leading into the woods.

Holmes paid the fare and added a generous tip.

"Before I go," Holmes said, "is there a police constable nearby?"

"Constable Barrow, sir. His cottage is down in the village, first one past the church."

"I know it's late, but would you be so kind as to inform him where I have gone? Tell him it concerns a missing person and I have reason to believe they may be inside the Redfords' former home, possibly being held against their will."

The cabman's expression grew serious. "Right away, sir."

Holmes watched the cab turn and head back down the hill before he set off along the path. The only light he had to guide him was the full moon, which cast an eerie silver glow through the bare branches above. The path twisted through trees, climbing steadily. Twice he heard rustling in the undergrowth, causing him to pause and listen intently before continuing.

His mind raced with possibilities. If Watson had been taken by Sarah Redford, what state would he be in? Had she acted alone or with accomplices? Holmes mentally prepared for several scenarios, each more concerning than the last.

The path finally opened onto a small clearing. There stood the cottage, a modest structure which now bore the marks of neglect. Ivy had claimed one wall entirely. Several slate tiles had slipped from the roof, and one of the windows was boarded over. The small garden that fronted the property had long ago surrendered to the wilderness.

Holmes paused at the edge of the clearing. Thin smoke rose from the chimney, nearly invisible against the dark sky. Someone was inside, then. A faint light flickered behind drawn curtains.

He decided on the direct approach towards the front door. Taking a deep breath, he moved forward silently, careful to avoid twigs or debris that might announce his presence. As he reached the garden gate, its rusty hinges protested loudly, the screech cutting through the quiet night. Holmes froze, listening for any reaction from within the cottage.

Holmes had taken three steps toward the door when it opened. A young woman emerged, her face pale and drawn in the moonlight. She wore a plain dark dress, her brown hair pulled back severely from her face. In her right hand, she held a revolver, pointed steadily at Holmes.

"Not another step," she said. "Mr Sherlock Holmes, I presume."

Holmes raised his hands slowly. "I am. And I believe you are Miss Sarah Redford. I have come about Dr Watson."

"I thought you might." Her voice was cold, devoid of emotion. "He said you would find us eventually. He was certain of it."

The mention of Watson sent a surge of hope through Holmes.

"Walk towards me and go inside. Slowly," Sarah commanded.

Holmes obeyed. Sarah stood to one side of the door, and he stepped inside. He felt the press of the revolver against his back. He was in a small sitting room. A fire burned low in the grate, casting weak light over furniture draped with dust sheets. The air was damp and smelled of mould and smoke.

"Sit there," Sarah said, forcing him towards a wooden chair positioned near the fireplace.

Holmes sat, taking the opportunity to observe her more closely. She was thin to the point of gauntness, with dark circles under her eyes suggesting many sleepless nights. Most disturbing were the dark stains on the cuffs of her sleeves which were unmistakably dried blood. Holmes felt a chill at the sight but maintained his composure.

"Where is Watson?" Holmes asked quietly.

"Concerned for your friend, Mr Holmes? How touching." She kept the revolver trained on him as she moved to stand before the fireplace. "He's alive. For now."

"I would like to see him."

"I'm sure you would." She tilted her head, studying him. "The great detective, come to the rescue. Just as Dr Watson predicted. He told me you would find us, no matter where we went. He was quite confident about it."

Holmes remained outwardly calm, though internally he was cataloguing every detail of the room, searching for clues about Watson's location and condition. The blood on Sarah's cuffs was concerning, but not necessarily fatal. The layout of the cottage suggested limited space. Watson had to be nearby.

"Justice has already begun," Sarah continued, a disturbing gleam in her eyes.

Holmes kept his voice level. "Justice for what, precisely?"

Sarah's eyes flashed with anger. "For my father. And for fifteen years of watching my mother waste away from grief.

For the life we should have had before Dr Watson took it all away."

"I have read Dr Watson's journal concerning your father. Watson did everything he could to save him."

"That's a lie!" The revolver trembled in her hand. "He killed my father just as surely as if he'd administered poison. He was incompetent, or negligent, or both. And he's never faced consequences for it. Never had to live with the ruin he caused."

"What have you done to him?" Holmes asked.

"Nothing he hasn't deserved," she replied. "But don't worry. I want him to suffer slowly. I want him to understand what he's done. Death would be too quick, too merciful."

Holmes glanced around the room, looking for any sign of Watson or where he might be held. His mind worked methodically through possible strategies. Confrontation seemed unwise given the revolver. Reasoning with Sarah might be possible, but her emotional state appeared volatile. He needed more information, to play for time.

"Your mother has recently passed away. That must have been difficult for you."

A shadow crossed Sarah's face. "She died still waiting for justice. Still believing that one day, Watson would answer for what he did. And now he will."

"This will not bring your father back, Miss Redford. Nor would he wish to see his daughter become a criminal."

"Don't speak of my father!" Sarah's hand tightened on the revolver. "You didn't know him. You don't know what he would want."

"I know he was a doctor, like Watson. A man dedicated to preserving life, not taking it. I'll ask again, where is Dr Watson?"

"Close enough to hear us. Close enough to know that his great friend Sherlock Holmes can't help him now."

Holmes glanced toward a closed door at the far end of the room. Sarah followed his gaze and smiled.

"Very good, Mr Holmes. Your powers of deduction remain intact." She stepped closer, the revolver now inches from his chest. "But they won't save either of you."

Chapter 9

Holmes regarded Sarah Redford with careful attention. Her frame was slight, yet the steady hand that held the pistol betrayed a determination that belied her fragile appearance.

"Miss Redford," Holmes said, his voice deliberately calm, "perhaps you might explain why you hold Dr Watson responsible for your father's death."

"I've already told you!"

"I would like to hear a more detailed account of it," Holmes said. "Even though I appreciate how distressing this is for you."

"Father was ill. Not seriously at first. Fatigue, some weight loss. Well, this is all according to my mother. Dr Watson was a colleague of Father's. We had no reason to doubt him. Yet all the remedies he tried didn't have any effect. In fact, they made him worse, much worse. My father wasted away before our eyes."

"Do you believe Dr Watson should have done more?" Holmes prompted, cataloguing the distance to the door, the uneven floorboards between them, and the slight tremor in Sarah's hand that had not been there moments ago.

"Done more?" Sarah's voice rose sharply. "He should have saved him! Instead, he watched as my father grew confused and weaker. He watched as my father slipped away from us. Oh yes, he could have done a lot more!"

"Medicine is an imperfect science, Miss Redford," Holmes said. "Even the most skilled physician cannot always save a patient."

"Spare me your defences," Sarah spat. "Mother knew. She knew Dr Watson was incompetent or negligent or worse. She told me so every day until her own death. And now, finally, Dr Watson will pay for what he did. He's in the cellar. I persuaded him to go down the stairs. Alas, he took a tumble down them and hit his head."

Holmes' gaze fell to the rust-coloured stains on her sleeves. "Is that why you have blood on you? Have you checked Dr Watson's injuries?"

"I did. He is alive. For now. Soon enough, he will know what it is to suffer as my father did. To be abandoned and left to die."

"He requires medical attention," Holmes said. "Surely you don't intend to let him perish in the cellar?"

"That is precisely my intention. An eye for an eye. A doctor for a doctor. Justice, of a sort."

Holmes noted the increasing wildness in her eyes, the slight unsteadiness in her stance. The grief of her father's death, compounded by her mother's recent passing, had clearly unhinged her mind.

"And what of your own life, Miss Redford? Have you considered the consequences of such an action?"

"My life ended fifteen years ago," she replied. "The day my father died and my mother's heart turned to stone. I have existed merely to see this day come."

Holmes maintained his gaze on her face but was acutely aware of the sounds outside. A distant crunch of gravel. The soft whisper of footsteps approaching the cottage. The local constable, perhaps, alerted by the cab driver he had spoken to earlier.

Sarah was warming to her theme. "It was so easy to lure your friend here. I sent a telegram, claiming a child was gravely ill and needed immediate medical attention. Then I waited in a cab near Rose Lane. He came just as I knew he would. I called out his name and made up something about having a poorly child in the cab. As soon as he came nearer, I aimed my pistol at him and ordered him into the cab."

"And the journey here?" Holmes said. "He must have realised something was amiss."

"I had the gun against his side the entire journey," Sarah said, a disturbing pride in her voice. "I paid the cab driver handsomely from my savings, enough to ensure his silence and to bring us all the way from London."

"Watson would have tried to reason with you," Holmes said, watching her carefully.

Sarah's lips curled into a bitter smile. "Oh, he did. He spoke of his regret about Father, claiming he had done everything possible to save him. He even offered to review Father's case again, to see if modern medicine might reveal what had afflicted him. As if that would bring Father back! I told him if he made any attempt to signal for help or escape, I would shoot him there in the cab. The doctor became quite silent after that."

Holmes detected movement in his peripheral vision. A shadow passed by the broken window.

"Well, Miss Redford," he said, "I believe your careful planning may have overlooked one critical element."

Sarah frowned. "And what might that be?"

"Me." Holmes glanced sharply toward the still-closed door. He cried out, "Ah, there you are!"

The moment Sarah turned her head toward the phantom arrival, Holmes lunged from the chair. His hand closed around her wrist, forcing the pistol upward. Sarah shrieked in rage, her finger tightening on the trigger. The report was deafening in the small room as the bullet splintered the wooden beams above them.

They struggled, Sarah fighting with the desperate strength of madness. Holmes twisted her arm, his superior strength gradually overpowering her, but not before her knee connected with his stomach, driving the breath from his lungs.

The door burst open. Two constables rushed in, their heavy boots thundering on the floorboards.

"Seize her!" Holmes gasped, finally wrenching the pistol from Sarah's grasp.

The officers took hold of Sarah, who continued to thrash and scream. "He deserves to die! My father's blood is on his hands!"

Holmes handed the weapon to the senior officer. "This woman has kidnapped Dr Watson. He's injured and being held in the cellar. I must see to him."

The constable nodded. "We'll handle this young lady, sir."

Without waiting for further discussion, Holmes rushed to the door Sarah had indicated earlier. He flung it open to reveal a narrow staircase descending into darkness. He took the stairs two at a time, the dank smell of earth and mildew growing stronger with each step.

"Watson!" he called. "Watson, can you hear me?"

At the bottom of the stairs, Holmes' eyes adjusted to the gloom. The cellar was small, with a dirt floor and stone walls slick with moisture. In the far corner, slumped against the cold stone, was the familiar form of his friend.

Watson lay motionless, his head tilted at an unnatural angle. A dark stain had spread across the collar of his shirt, and a trail of dried blood ran from a wound at his temple down the side of his face.

Holmes crossed the space in three strides, dropping to his knees beside the doctor. He pressed his fingers to Watson's neck, desperately searching for a pulse.

Chapter 10

A pale light illuminated the sparse hospital room where Holmes kept his unwavering watch. The morning had arrived with little fanfare, the grey dawn matching Holmes' mood as he studied Watson's still form on the narrow bed.

The small provincial hospital had done what it could for Watson after Holmes had found him unconscious in the cellar of the derelict cottage. The local doctor had worked diligently to clean and dress the wound, muttering grave concerns about concussion and the dangers of prolonged unconsciousness. That had been hours ago, and still, Watson had not stirred.

Holmes had refused all offers of accommodation, choosing instead to remain in the straight-backed wooden chair beside Watson's bed. He had spent the night watching his friend for any signs of movement, mentally reconstructing the sequence of events that had led to this moment, and contemplating the bitter hatred that had festered in Sarah Redford for fifteen long years.

He had sent a telegram to Mrs Hudson to let her know Watson had been found and was somewhat injured. He hadn't gone into details about the extent of Watson's injuries and only reported that the doctor was being looked after in a hospital. He would give Mrs Hudson the full details when he returned to London.

The sound of footsteps in the corridor broke his concentration. The door opened to admit a doctor, not the young man who had treated Watson initially, but an older, more authoritative figure. His greying whiskers were neatly trimmed, and round spectacles sat upon his nose. He carried a clipboard and wore the weary expression of a man who had seen too many injuries in his time.

"Good morning," he said. "I am Dr Harrington. I have taken over Dr Watson's care. I understand you are Sherlock Holmes." His gaze swept over Holmes, noting the rumpled clothing and the dark shadows beneath his eyes. "Have you been here all night?"

Holmes replied, "I have."

"You must have had some rest surely?" The doctor moved to the opposite side of the bed and began to check Watson's pulse.

"No," Holmes replied. "Sleep is unnecessary at present."

Dr Harrington frowned as he made a notation on his clipboard. "Every man requires sleep, Mr Holmes. You cannot function properly without it. I would strongly advise—"

A soft voice from the bed interrupted their exchange. "I can attest that Holmes functions quite admirably without days of sleep. I have witnessed it on numerous occasions."

Holmes straightened immediately. "Watson!"

Watson's eyes were open, though clouded with confusion. He attempted to raise himself from the pillows but winced visibly and fell back with a groan.

"Please remain still, Dr Watson," Harrington said, placing a restraining hand on Watson's shoulder. "You have suffered a significant injury."

Watson licked his dry lips. "Water," he whispered.

Holmes stood and reached for the glass on the bedside table. He carefully supported Watson's head as he drank.

"Where am I?" Watson asked once he had taken a few sips.

"You are in Dorking Hospital," Holmes answered. "Do you recall how you came to be here?"

Watson answered, "I remember receiving a telegram, yesterday I think. It was barely light." He paused, each word seemingly a great effort. "A child was gravely ill in Clerkenwell. Thirty-three Rose Lane, I believe. I went there immediately, but there was no ill child."

"And then?" Holmes prompted gently.

"A young woman called to me from a hansom cab," Watson continued, his voice growing stronger as the memory returned. "She claimed to know me. When I approached, she said, oh, what did she say? Oh yes, that was it. She asked me to examine someone in the cab. But there wasn't anyone else inside but her. And then she..." He stopped abruptly, his hand moving instinctively to his bandaged head.

Dr Harrington held his hand up. "This questioning must cease at once," he said firmly to Holmes. "Dr Watson has suffered a serious concussion. He requires absolute rest and quiet."

Holmes chose to ignore him and said, "Watson, you have been unconscious since yesterday. I found you in the cellar of a derelict cottage near Box Hill."

"Really?" Watson declared. "What was I doing there?"

Dr Harrington made an exasperated sound. "This is precisely the sort of excitement I wished to avoid. Mr Holmes, you must leave immediately."

Holmes said, "One question more, and then I shall depart. Watson, do you recall a Dr Redford who was under your care but died some fifteen years ago?"

Watson's face grew troubled. "Redford?" he repeated slowly. "The name stirs something, something unpleasant." His eyes suddenly widened with recognition. "A difficult case. He should not have died. I tried everything."

"His daughter," Holmes prompted. "Do you recall her?"

"A child," Watson murmured. "Ten years old, perhaps. Quiet, observant." His expression changed suddenly. "It was her! The woman in the cab. She had a pisto. It was Dr Redford's daughter!"

"Yes, it was, " Holmes confirmed. "Sarah Redford has harboured a belief that you were somehow responsible for her father's death. That belief, nurtured by her mother over years, drove her to seek revenge."

Watson struggled to sit up, agitation clear in his movements. "That is absurd! I did everything medically possible for Dr Redford. Did you find my journal, Holmes? I dropped it without Miss Redford noticing, hoping you would find it."

"I did find it," Holmes confirmed. "And it started a change of events that led me to you. Watson, can I ask–"

"You must leave now, Mr Holmes," Dr Harrington interrupted, his patience clearly exhausted. "You have asked more than enough questions. My patient is becoming distressed, which could have serious consequences for his recovery. If you do not leave this instant, I shall be forced to summon the police to remove you from the premises."

Holmes gathered his coat with deliberate calm. "Very well. I shall return to London, but I will come back later." He paused, his expression softening almost imperceptibly. "My dear Watson, I do not for one moment believe you were responsible for Dr Redford's death. I shall uncover the truth of this matter."

Watson nodded weakly, but his eyes were already closing with exhaustion. "The medical records," he murmured. "Check my notes on the case. They might help."

"I already have," Holmes said. "Now you must rest."

As Holmes departed, Dr Harrington moved to adjust Watson's pillow and check his bandages.

Holmes strode from the hospital, the morning air brisk against his face. The accusation against Watson was preposterous, yet Sarah Redford's conviction had been powerful enough to drive her to violence. There was more to this case than met the eye, and Holmes was determined to discover what truly happened to Dr Redford all those years ago. The truth, he was certain, would exonerate his friend completely.

With renewed purpose, Holmes pulled his coat tighter against the chill and set out to find transport back to London.

Chapter 11

The train journey from Dorking to London provided Holmes with ample time to decide on his next course of action. He would revisit the Redfords' former home and speak with any longstanding residents who might have observed the family fifteen years ago. Mrs Redford's landlady had mentioned a man who had handled the sale of the Redford house, this man being a friend of the late Dr Redford. Maybe someone knew who that was.

The train came to a stop and Holmes disembarked. When he arrived at the row of townhouses where the Redfords had once lived, he began his inquiries methodically, moving from house to house and knocking on the doors.

"I regret we cannot help you," said one resident. "We purchased the property only seven years ago."

Another replied, "The Redfords? The name sounds vaguely familiar, but I cannot recall anything specific about them."

After several similarly fruitless conversations, Holmes noticed something curious. A curtain twitched in a window of the house directly opposite the former Redford residence. Each time he glanced in that direction, a female figure hastily withdrew from view. This covert observation continued as Holmes knocked on neighbouring doors, too deliberate to be coincidental.

Holmes crossed the street and approached the house in question. The curtain moved again as he mounted the steps. He rapped on the door, which opened almost immediately to reveal a woman in her late thirties. She possessed a round, kind face framed by brown hair, and her eyes held intelligence and curiosity.

"Mr Sherlock Holmes," she said, surprising him with her immediate recognition. "I thought it might be you. I have read about you in the newspapers. The journalists described you well."

Holmes inclined his head in greeting and said, "You have been watching me."

The woman laughed. "I have indeed. Dreadfully nosy of me, I know. My husband always says curiosity will be my undoing."

"Not nosy at all," Holmes replied. "Merely observant. I often find myself looking out of windows at the world beyond. It is remarkable what one may learn through such observation."

"How delightful to hear someone else say so," she responded. "I am Mrs Atkins. Please do come in. I suspect you have questions about this street. I saw you talking to my neighbours. I have lived here for twenty years, and as you have witnessed, I am very observant."

Holmes followed Mrs Atkins into a comfortable sitting room. His attention was immediately drawn to a bookshelf filled with detective novels. He recognised works by Wilkie Collins, Émile Gaboriau, and Anna Katharine Green arranged prominently alongside more recent publications.

"You enjoy mysteries," Holmes said.

"Passionately," Mrs Atkins confirmed as she gestured for him to sit. "Though I must say, the cases described in your friend Dr Watson's accounts surpass anything in fiction."

Holmes sat in the offered chair. "Mrs Atkins, I am investigating a matter concerning the Redford family who used to live across the street. Did you know them well?"

"Not intimately, but well enough for neighbours," she replied. "Dr Redford seemed a pleasant gentleman, always courteous when we passed on the street. Mrs Redford was more reserved, though perfectly civil. They had a daughter, a quiet child who barely left the side of her mother."

"You mentioned you have lived here for twenty years. Were you present during Dr Redford's illness fifteen years ago?"

Mrs Atkins nodded gravely. "I was, and in a unique position to observe the comings and goings at their house. I often saw your Dr Watson arriving and going inside. But I also observed something else, something peculiar. You see, my youngest son was a newborn at the time, and he suffered terribly from colic. I spent many nights awake, pacing before the windows with him in my arms, trying to soothe his discomfort. Nothing would settle him except movement and seeing the glow of the gaslights outside, so I would often walk past the windows which gave me a clear view of the street."

Holmes asked, "And during these sleepless nights, did you notice anything unusual across the street?"

"I did." Mrs Atkins rose and moved to a small desk in the corner of the room. From a drawer, she withdrew a leather-bound book. "I kept a household ledger where I recorded my son's feeding schedule and sleep patterns during those terrible times. Some instinct also made me record details of that visitor to the Redfords' home during those late hours. Perhaps I've been reading too many detective novels and view everyone as being of a suspicious nature!"

She opened the ledger and placed it before Holmes. "Here, you see? On four separate occasions, a man called Dr Wicklow entered the Redford house well past midnight. He let himself in with a key."

Holmes examined the entries, committing them to memory. He said, "You are certain it was Dr Wicklow?"

"Absolutely certain," Mrs Atkins replied firmly. "I had previous experience with the man when he treated my eldest son for a broken arm. He was cold, dismissive, and charged an exorbitant fee for what I considered inadequate care. I would not mistake him for another."

"Did you ever mention these visits to Mrs Redford?"

"No," Mrs Atkins admitted. "It seemed improper to intrude upon their private affairs. Besides, I assumed Dr Wicklow was consulting on Dr Redford's case, despite the unusual timing."

"What happened after Dr Redford's death?" Holmes inquired.

"It seems Dr Wicklow took charge of everything," Mrs Atkins replied. "I visited Mrs Redford to offer my condolences, and she mentioned that Dr Wicklow was handling all financial matters, including the sale of their home. She seemed grateful for his assistance."

"Did she mention the proceeds from this sale?"

"Yes, and it troubled me greatly," Mrs Atkins said. "She told me the house had sold for much less than expected, forcing them into reduced circumstances. She quoted a figure that seemed impossibly low for this area, even then. I did not contradict her, not wishing to cause further distress."

"Do you know the nature of Dr Redford's relationship with Dr Wicklow beyond these nocturnal visits?"

"They were business partners in a medical practice," Mrs Atkins informed him. "Dr Redford mentioned it once when we conversed about his work. I thought it was a strange partnership, although I didn't voice my opinion, of course. Dr Redford was so kind and caring, and Dr Wicklow quite the opposite. I do not know what became of the practice after his death."

"Mrs Atkins, you mentioned that Dr Wicklow handled the sale of the Redford house. Do you know which estate agent he employed for this transaction?"

"Indeed I do," she replied with evident distaste. "A most unpleasant man called Arthur Tattersall. He has pestered me repeatedly over the years, trying to persuade me to sell my home. There is something about him that I thoroughly distrust."

"Your instincts are sound," Holmes said. "I have encountered Mr Tattersall before in connection with questionable business practices. He is known to associate with individuals of dubious character."

Mrs Atkins looked vindicated. "I knew it! There is a certain manner about truly dishonest people that one can sense, do you not think?"

"You possess remarkable powers of observation," Holmes said sincerely. "You have the makings of an excellent detective."

"What a delightful compliment," she replied with a smile. "My husband insists I simply have an overactive imagination fuelled by too many sensational novels."

Holmes rose to take his leave. "Thank you for your assistance. You have provided valuable information."

"I hope it helps resolve whatever matter brought you here. I am more than happy to officially confirm those sightings of Dr Wicklow, if that would help you." She showed him to the door. "Will I read about this case in The Strand someday?"

"Perhaps," Holmes replied. "Though Dr Watson tends to exercise considerable discretion in which cases he decides to publicise."

As Holmes departed Mrs Atkins' home, his mind worked to connect the new information with what he already knew. Wicklow's late-night visits during Redford's illness, his management of the family's financial affairs, and his connection to the unscrupulous Tattersall suggested a troubling pattern.

The implications were disturbing. Could Wicklow have deceived Mrs Redford about the sale price, pocketing the difference himself? More disturbingly, might he have had a more sinister role in Redford's death? The alibi Wicklow had provided for the day of Watson's abduction was solid, but that did not preclude earlier deceptions.

It was time to pay a visit to Mr Arthur Tattersall, a man who might hold crucial answers about what had truly happened to Dr Harold Redford fifteen years ago.

Chapter 12

Holmes found Arthur Tattersall's offices in a handsome stone building near Chancery Lane. The location projected an air of respectability, with gleaming brass fixtures on the door and an imposing marble entrance hall. A directory in the foyer listed 'Tattersall Estate Agency' on the third floor, alongside the names of several solicitors and financial consultants.

As Holmes climbed the staircase, he observed the polished oak bannisters and expensive carpeting. Tattersall clearly wished to present himself as a successful, established businessman. Holmes knew this carefully constructed image concealed more questionable enterprises.

The third-floor corridor was quiet, save for the muffled sounds of typewriters and conversations behind closed doors. Holmes approached a frosted glass door bearing Tattersall's name in elegant gold lettering. Before he could knock, the door opened, and two men emerged.

Holmes recognised them instantly. The shorter man was Samuel Brock, a known fence for stolen jewellery. The taller, broad-shouldered individual was James Harker, who had been implicated in several protection rackets across Southwark. Both men glanced at Holmes, recognition flashing in their eyes before they hurriedly looked away and quickened their pace toward the stairs.

Holmes smiled slightly at their discomfort. His presence clearly unsettled them, suggesting their business with Tattersall was not entirely legitimate. He waited until they had descended the stairs before entering the estate agent's office.

A young clerk looked up from his typewriter. "May I help you, sir?"

"I wish to speak with Mr Tattersall on a matter of some urgency," Holmes replied.

"Do you have an appointment? Mr Tattersall is extremely busy today."

"I do not, but I believe he will want to speak with me nonetheless." Holmes handed the clerk his card. "Please inform him that Sherlock Holmes desires a few moments of his time."

The clerk rose from his desk and disappeared through an inner door. Holmes heard a murmur of voices, followed by a sharp exclamation. A moment later, the clerk returned.

"Mr Tattersall will see you, sir. Please, follow me."

Holmes was shown into a spacious office that spoke of calculated opulence. The furniture was expensive but not ostentatious, the sort chosen to impress clients of a certain class without appearing vulgar. The walls featured framed certificates and photographs of notable London buildings.

Arthur Tattersall sat behind a substantial mahogany desk. He was a man in his fifties, immaculately dressed in a charcoal suit that had been fashionable perhaps five years earlier. His silver hair was precisely parted, and his moustache had been waxed to perfect points. A gold watch chain stretched across his waistcoat.

"Sherlock Holmes," Tattersall said, his voice cold. "I remember you quite well. The Crossfield matter, was it not? I believe your interference in that sale cost me a considerable commission."

"The courts ultimately found the documents had been altered," Holmes replied calmly, taking the seat opposite without waiting for an invitation. "A most unfortunate discovery for all involved."

Tattersall's jaw tightened. "What brings you to my office? I am exceedingly busy today."

"I require information about a property transaction you handled fifteen years ago," Holmes said. "A townhouse in Marylebone belonging to Dr Harold Redford."

"Fifteen years is a considerable time, Mr Holmes. I cannot be expected to recall every transaction from so long ago."

"I suspect this particular sale might be memorable," Holmes replied. "It was handled by a colleague of Dr Redford, a man named Dr Nathaniel Wicklow."

"As I said, I handle numerous transactions. If there are specific details you require, perhaps my clerk can search the archives."

Holmes persisted. "Mr Tattersall, I am conducting an investigation into a serious matter that has resulted in harm to a close associate of mine who knew Dr Redford. I suspect the sale of Dr Redford's house may not have been entirely legitimate and this information is relevant to my investigation."

"That is a very serious accusation, Mr Holmes," Tattersall said, his face hardening. "I conduct my business according to the letter of the law."

"Of course," Holmes replied smoothly. "Which is why I am certain you will have no objection to showing me the documents related to this transaction. For the sake of clarity, you understand."

"I am under no obligation to share confidential business records with you. You have no official standing."

Holmes nodded thoughtfully. "True. Perhaps Inspector Lestrade would have better luck. He would be greatly interested in a property transaction involving a suspicious death."

Tattersall's face remained impassive, but Holmes noticed a slight sheen of perspiration on his brow.

"I could have him here within the hour," Holmes continued. "He would be most interested to meet with Brock and Harker as well. I saw them leaving as I arrived. Though perhaps their business with you was entirely legitimate."

The estate agent studied Holmes for a long moment. "What exactly do you want, Mr Holmes?"

"Access to the complete records of the Redford property sale. Nothing more."

Tattersall hesitated, then rose from his chair. He crossed to a cabinet, unlocked it with a key from his waistcoat pocket, and withdrew a leather portfolio. "These are confidential business documents, Mr Holmes. I trust you will treat them accordingly."

"I am interested solely in the facts they contain," Holmes assured him, accepting the portfolio and opening it carefully.

The documents inside told a disturbing story. The sale agreement presented to Mrs Redford showed a purchase price of fourteen hundred pounds, while the actual transaction recorded with the Land Registry listed thirty-two hundred pounds. The difference had been concealed through a series of complex manoeuvres involving rapid resale and supposed improvements to the property.

"A significant discrepancy," Holmes observed. "And all matters were agreed by Dr Wicklow."

"The arrangement was entirely legal," Tattersall said stiffly. "Dr Wicklow had power of attorney to act on Mrs Redford's behalf."

"Did Mrs Redford know the true sale price?"

"My dealings were exclusively with Dr Wicklow," Tattersall replied. "He assured me that Mrs Redford wished to conclude matters quickly and with minimal involvement."

"I see. And the medical practice? I understand Dr Redford was partners with Dr Wicklow. Did you have anything to do with that?"

A flicker of surprise crossed Tattersall's face. "You seem remarkably well-informed."

"Were you involved in the transfer of Dr Redford's share of the practice as well?"

Tattersall nodded reluctantly. "There was a provision in their partnership agreement that in the event of one partner's death, the other would purchase the deceased's share at a predetermined value."

"Which was?"

"Dr Wicklow acquired Dr Redford's share for eight hundred pounds."

"And its true value?"

Tattersall hesitated before answering. "The practice was sold in its entirety a year later for nearly five thousand pounds."

Holmes removed several documents from the portfolio. "I require copies of these papers."

"That is out of the question," Tattersall protested. "I have already shown you more than I should."

"Mr Tattersall," Holmes said, "a man has died, and another has been grievously injured as a direct result of events set in motion fifteen years ago. I can either leave here with copies of these documents, or I can return with Inspector Lestrade and a warrant, at which point all of your files will be subject to examination. Which would you prefer?"

Without any hesitation, the estate agent rang for his clerk and instructed the young man to make copies of the documents Holmes had selected.

"It may take some time," he said.

"I am in no hurry," Holmes replied, settling more comfortably in his chair.

An uncomfortable silence fell between them, broken only by the ticking of an ornate clock on the mantelpiece. Holmes did not attempt conversation, knowing that Tattersall's discomfort would only increase with each passing minute.

The clerk returned with the copies, which Holmes examined carefully before placing them in his coat pocket.

"Thank you for your cooperation, Mr Tattersall," Holmes said as he rose to leave. "I trust our conversation will remain between us."

"Of course," Tattersall replied stiffly. "Though I maintain that everything was handled legally."

"The law and justice are not always perfectly aligned," Holmes observed. "Good day, Mr Tattersall."

Holmes departed, leaving the estate agent seated at his desk, visibly unsettled.

The documents had confirmed his suspicions about Wicklow's duplicity in financial matters. The doctor had systematically defrauded Mrs Redford while posing as her advocate and friend. Such behaviour cast a troubling light on his potential involvement in Redford's death as well.

Holmes needed more evidence, and he knew where to look for it.

Chapter 13

A while later, Holmes approached the entrance to St Thomas' Hospital. He had already visited it the previous day to confirm Dr Wicklow's alibi for the morning of the abduction. On that occasion, he had spoken with the young duty doctor and a junior nurse, both of whom had verified Wicklow's presence during surgery. Now Holmes returned with more specific questions and a growing suspicion that Wicklow's misdeeds extended far beyond financial fraud.

Holmes entered the hospital and made his way to the surgical wing. The corridors were busy with nurses and orderlies moving purposefully between wards. The antiseptic smell hung in the air, mingling with the unmistakable odours of illness and suffering that permeated all hospitals despite the best efforts of the staff.

At the nurses' station, Holmes found a middle-aged woman dressed in a uniform. The gentle authority with which she directed a young probationer suggested considerable experience and seniority.

"Pardon me," Holmes said politely to the woman. "I am looking for Dr Wicklow."

The nurse's expression was professionally neutral. "May I ask who is inquiring?"

"My name is Sherlock Holmes. I am investigating a matter in which Dr Wicklow may be able to assist."

"I see. Dr Wicklow is away until tomorrow. Is there something I can help you with? I am Sister Margaret Campbell."

"Do you know Dr Wicklow well?"

"I have worked with Dr Wicklow for nearly twenty years if that answers your question."

"It does," Holmes said. "You may be able to help me. I have several questions about Dr Wicklow's practices."

"What sort of practices?"

"His surgical techniques, his patient care, his record-keeping." Holmes watched her closely. "His use of hospital medicines and supplies."

Sister Campbell glanced around the busy corridor. "Perhaps we should speak somewhere more private."

She led him to a small office, closing the door behind them. The room contained a table, several chairs, and shelves lined with medical textbooks and journals. The nurse took a seat and Holmes sat opposite her.

"Why are you asking about Dr Wicklow?" Sister Campbell asked.

"I am investigating a serious matter and a suspicious death," Holmes replied simply, choosing not to elaborate.

Sister Campbell paled visibly. "I don't know anything about such matters. Dr Wicklow is a senior physician at this hospital. Any accusation against him would require substantial evidence."

"Which is precisely what I am seeking," Holmes said. "You have worked with him for many years. Surely you have observed his methods, his habits."

"I have done my duty," she replied stiffly. "Nothing more."

Holmes noted the slight tremor in her hands and the tension in her shoulders. "You are afraid of him," he stated rather than asked.

Sister Campbell did not answer immediately. When she spoke, her voice was much quieter. "If I were to speak against Dr Wicklow, I would never work as a nurse again. He has influence, and connections. He would ensure I was dismissed and that no other hospital would employ me. I have seen him do exactly that to other members of staff who have crossed him."

"I understand your concern," Holmes said gently. "But I must tell you that I have reason to believe that Dr Wicklow may be behind the death of a colleague. What can you tell me about Dr Wicklow's methods?"

Sister Campbell said, "I must admit, there have been irregularities over the years. Unusual prescriptions. Unexpected complications with certain patients, even unexpected deaths. But nothing I could definitively point to as wrongdoing. However, these incidents always seem to involve Dr Wicklow and not the other doctors. But perhaps they are merely coincidences."

"I don't believe in those," Holmes said. "There must be evidence to prove these irregularities concerning Dr Wicklow, and I need your help to find that evidence. From what you've told me, your patients could be at risk."

The nurse looked at Holmes for a few moments and then said, "If I assist you, will you protect my identity? I have elderly parents to support. I cannot risk losing my position. But more importantly, I cannot live with myself if patients are being harmed by Dr Wicklow and I had the power to stop it."

"You have my word," Holmes promised. "I will not reveal the source of any information you provide."

Sister Campbell seemed to come to a decision. "I can let you into Dr Wicklow's office. He keeps his records in there. I have a key to his office."

"Then perhaps we might examine those private records," Holmes suggested. "If they contain nothing incriminating, no one need ever know we looked."

Sister Campbell looked as if she might change her mind, but then stood abruptly and said, "Follow me. But we must be discreet."

She led Holmes to a section of the surgical wing that seemed less frequented. They passed several closed doors before stopping at one bearing a brass nameplate: 'Dr N. Wicklow, Senior Consulting Surgeon.'

Sister Campbell removed a ring of keys from her pocket and unlocked the door, glancing nervously in both directions before ushering Holmes inside. The office was immaculately kept, with leather-bound medical texts arranged precisely on shelves, surgical diagrams framed on the walls, and a large desk free of clutter.

"That cabinet is where Dr Wicklow keeps his records," Sister Campbell said, pointing to a tall oak cabinet in the corner. "I don't have a key to that."

"We don't need one," Holmes said. He made swift work of utilising a tool from his inside pocket to unlock the cabinet. He examined the ledgers on the top shelf and asked if it was normal for the hospital doctors to have two ledgers for each year.

"No, it isn't," Sister Campbell replied, moving closer.

She took two ledgers out that had the latest year written on the spines. She placed them on the desk and opened them. With Holmes at her side, they soon worked out that one ledger was for official hospital records while the other one seemed to be for Wicklow's eyes only.

Sister Campbell shook her head. "I don't understand. Why would he have two ledgers? I can see that one refers to his patients at this hospital and the treatments they have received, but I can't make sense of the other one. There's a list of items in that one bought from a chemist in Croydon. We've never used such a chemist for our supplies. And why did Dr Wicklow have the items delivered to his home address? It doesn't make sense."

Holmes said, "What can you tell me about those items purchased from the Croydon chemist? Do you recognise them?"

Sister Cambell looked at the ledger in more detail. She said, "Some of these are new medications that haven't been widely tested yet and not something that would be used by our doctors. Some of the other items are toxic in nature and shouldn't be used on any patient, or any healthy person, in fact. What on earth was Dr Wicklow doing with these?"

Holmes chose his next words carefully. "Perhaps you should cross-reference the purchase of these unusual supplies against the date of any suspicious deaths that may have occurred at the hospital."

Sister Campbell looked up from the ledger and gave Holmes a long look. Holmes held her gaze and after a few seconds, he saw understanding dawning on her face.

"You don't mean to say...? She shook her head. "No, that's impossible. I don't believe it. Are you insinuating that Dr Wicklow has used some of these dubious medications on his patients? And that he may have killed them on purpose? But that's horrific! No one would do something like that! Especially not a respected physician like Doctor Wicklow."

Holmes said, "Yet, you did mention irregularities over the years." He let his words sink in.

"But he couldn't have possibly done such a thing." Sister Campbell fell silent for a few moments. Then she said, "Could he?"

"These records could provide the answer, albeit an answer you don't want. If I may, I would like to look through the records that are dated fifteen years ago. I have some information I'd like to share with you but I would appreciate it if you could keep this to yourself for now."

Sister Campbell said she would.

Holmes proceeded to tell her of the events from the last two days starting with how Watson had been abducted, and how Holmes' investigation had led him to the present moment. Sister Cambell listened without saying a word.

When Holmes had finished, she said, "Tell me more about Dr Watson's notes concerning Dr Redford. Don't leave anything out. The slightest detail could be important."

Holmes smiled. "That's what I normally say to people." He told her everything.

Sister Campbell then looked through Wicklow's private ledger and found the dates of Dr Redford's illness and subsequent death.

"Look," she pointed at the ledger. "A few weeks before Dr Redford fell ill, Dr Wicklow purchased a large amount of arsenic. After that, he made a list of dates with measurements of that arsenic and ticked each one. Based on what you've told me, Dr Wicklow could have been secretly administering these doses to Dr Redford. That would have resulted in Dr Redford's continual decline. No wonder Dr Watson's treatment wasn't effective. And you know what else this means, don't you?"

Holmes nodded. "The purchase of this arsenic took place before Dr Redford was even ill, so this murder, and we can call it murder, was planned."

Sister Campbell sighed. "I don't know what to say, I really don't. Where do we go from here? I can't stay silent, not while lives could be in danger. If Dr Wicklow did murder Dr Redford, which the evidence supports, has he killed other people? Patients at this very hospital?"

"You need to let the police know immediately," Holmes advised. "And you must keep these records safe. Dr Wicklow can't be allowed back into his office."

Sister Campbell raised her chin. "Dr Wicklow will not be allowed back into this hospital, never mind his office. The audacity of the man! I can't understand why he would do this, let alone keep recorded evidence right here in his office."

Holmes said, "People like Wicklow are arrogant enough to think they will never get caught. But that is about to change. Sister Campbell, I will go straight to Scotland Yard and speak to Inspector Lestrade. Can you keep these ledgers somewhere safe? I'm sure he will want to look at them. You said Dr Wicklow is away. Do you know where he is?"

"He's in Manchester but should be catching the overnight train back to London. Then he is going straight to the Royal College of Physicians to give a lecture."

"What is the subject of the lecture?" Holmes asked.

With not a flicker of emotion, Sister Campbell replied, "The Care and Wellbeing Of Our Patients."

Chapter 14

The lecture hall of the Royal College of Physicians was filled to capacity the following morning. Distinguished medical professionals in formal attire occupied nearly every seat, their attention fixed upon the figure standing at the podium. Dr Nathaniel Wicklow presented an imposing silhouette against the pale backdrop, his voice commanding as he addressed his colleagues.

"The relationship between physician and patient is sacred," Wicklow proclaimed, his words carrying to every corner of the hall. "Our first duty must always be to the welfare of those in our care. It is a responsibility we cannot take lightly."

He paused, surveying the audience with satisfaction as several heads nodded in agreement. The murmur of approval seemed to please him, and he continued with renewed vigour.

"In my thirty years of practice, I have witnessed remarkable advances in medical science. Yet the fundamental principle remains unchanged: we must earn the trust of our patients through unwavering dedication to their wellbeing."

As Wicklow elaborated upon his philosophy of patient care, the main doors at the rear of the hall opened quietly. Holmes entered, followed closely by Inspector Lestrade. Neither man took a seat. Instead, they remained at the back, Holmes studying Wicklow intently while Lestrade shifted uncomfortably beside him.

"Are you certain this is the proper venue?" Lestrade whispered, glancing at the assembled doctors. "Perhaps we should wait until the conclusion of his address."

"Justice has waited fifteen years already, Inspector," Holmes replied softly. "It shall wait no longer."

Wicklow continued, oblivious to their presence. "The modern physician must be vigilant against complacency. We must question our methods, review our diagnoses, and above all, maintain the highest ethical standards."

"How terribly ironic," Holmes muttered.

Wicklow gestured expansively. "I have found that meticulous record-keeping is essential to proper patient care.

One must document every treatment, every observation, every..."

"Every dose of poison administered, Dr Wicklow?"

Holmes' voice cut through the hall like a blade. A collective gasp rose from the audience as all heads turned toward him. Wicklow froze mid-gesture, his eyes narrowing as he identified the speaker.

"Mr Holmes," he said, his voice controlled despite the interruption. "This is hardly the appropriate forum for whatever eccentric theory you wish to propose."

Holmes strode down the central aisle, Lestrade following reluctantly in his wake. "On the contrary, it seems the perfect venue to discuss your particular approach to the medical profession. Your colleagues should be most interested to hear of your innovative methods."

A murmur rippled through the audience. The President of the College, a silver-haired gentleman seated at the side of the stage, rose with visible displeasure. "Sir, this is an outrage. You cannot simply interrupt..."

"I assure you," Holmes replied, "what I have to say is directly relevant to Dr Wicklow's discourse on patient care and ethical standards."

Wicklow's expression hardened. "Whatever accusation you intend to make, Mr Holmes, I suggest you consider the consequences most carefully. I have no time for your baseless insinuations."

Holmes reached the front of the hall and turned to face the audience. "I stand before you not with insinuations, but with evidence. Evidence concerning the death of Dr Harold Redford fifteen years ago."

Wicklow's face paled slightly. "Dr Redford's case was thoroughly documented. He died of a mysterious illness that defied treatment."

"It defied treatment," Holmes agreed, "because while Dr Watson attempted to cure him, you were systematically poisoning him with arsenic."

The audience erupted in shocked exclamations. The President called loudly for order, his voice barely audible above the commotion.

"This is slander!" Wicklow shouted over the commotion. "Leave at once, Mr Holmes!"

"The facts, Dr Wicklow, are these," Holmes continued implacably. "You and Dr Redford were partners in a medical practice. Upon his death, you acquired his share for a fraction of its value. You also orchestrated the sale of his home, collaborating with a disreputable estate agent to conceal the true purchase price from his widow. The difference, a substantial sum, no doubt found its way into your accounts. The financial improprieties, serious though they may be, pale in comparison to the murder itself."

Wicklow laughed, a harsh, brittle sound. "Murder? Have you taken leave of your senses? Redford died of natural causes. His death was regrettable but entirely..."

"Your private ledgers tell a different story," Holmes interjected. "The ledgers you kept in your office at St Thomas' Hospital, which detail your purchase of arsenic from a chemist in Croydon weeks before Dr Redford first displayed symptoms of illness."

A visible tremor passed through Wicklow's hands. "What ledgers? I don't know what you're talking about."

"The ones currently being examined by police specialists," Lestrade said. "Along with samples taken from the medicine cabinet in your home."

"This is absurd!" Wicklow exclaimed.

"You administered small doses of arsenic to Dr Redford over a period of weeks," Holmes said, addressing the audience as much as Wicklow. "Just enough to produce symptoms that might be attributed to a mysterious illness, but not enough to kill him outright. You even documented the doses in your private records, marking each one with a tick as it was administered. Most methodical."

Wicklow gripped the edges of the podium. "You have no proof. None whatsoever."

"Your meticulous nature has proved your undoing," Holmes replied. "While Dr Watson struggled to identify Redford's illness, you systematically increased the dosage. When Redford finally succumbed, you stepped in as the concerned colleague, offering to manage his affairs and support his family. In reality, you defrauded them of their inheritance while positioning yourself as their benefactor. Dr Wicklow, you were seen entering the Redfords' home many times during the night-time hours when Dr Redford was ill. I have a witness who will confirm this."

The audience was utterly silent now, every eye fixed on the confrontation unfolding before them.

"You cannot believe this madman," Wicklow appealed to his colleagues, desperation edging into his voice. "I have dedicated my life to medicine. I have served this institution faithfully for decades!"

"Your dedication to your own advancement is not in question," Holmes replied. "But we must also consider the curious pattern of unexpected deaths among patients under your care at St Thomas'. The police are looking into those incidents as we speak. They will also re-examine the death that occurred twenty years ago concerning the aristocrat's son, the incident that ended up in court. Perhaps you did get away with murder at that time despite Dr Watson testifying against you. You never truly forgave him, did you?"

Wicklow opened his mouth to speak and then closed it again. He looked away from his colleagues who were now staring at him.

"I believe we have heard enough," Lestrade announced, stepping forward. "Dr Nathaniel Wicklow, I am arresting you on suspicion of the murder of Dr Harold Redford."

Two constables who had been waiting at the back of the hall now moved forward to flank Wicklow. The doctor glared at Holmes with undisguised hatred as Lestrade continued.

"We shall also be investigating other suspicious deaths among your patients. The evidence already collected from your office and home is substantial."

Wicklow's composure finally cracked. "You had no right to enter my office or my home! This is persecution, nothing more!" Turning to the audience, he appealed once more to his colleagues. "You know me! You have worked alongside me for years! Surely you cannot believe these fantastic accusations!"

His plea was met with uncomfortable silence. The President had ceased attempting to restore order and now sat with his head bowed, as if unable to witness Wicklow's disgrace.

"Come along, Dr Wicklow," Lestrade said firmly. "We shall continue this discussion at Scotland Yard."

As the constables led Wicklow from the podium, he maintained his protestations of innocence, his voice growing more strident with each step. The audience watched in stunned silence as one of their most esteemed colleagues was escorted from the hall.

Holmes turned to address the assembly once more. "I apologise for the disruption to your proceedings. It was necessary to confront Dr Wicklow publicly to prevent any possibility of flight. The evidence against him is considerable."

As Holmes and Lestrade departed, the hall erupted into agitated discussion. The medical community would need time to process the shocking revelation about one of their most prominent members.

"It seems," Lestrade observed as they stepped outside, "that even the most respected among us can harbour the darkest secrets."

"Indeed," Holmes replied. "The evidence against Wicklow is overwhelming. His career of deception has finally come to an end. Now, if you will excuse me, Inspector, I must send a telegram to Dr Watson who is still in the hospital in Dorking. He deserves to know the full truth of this matter."

Lestrade nodded. "Of course. I shall see you later at Scotland Yard to complete the formal statements."

They parted ways and Holmes headed towards the nearest telegram office. His thoughts turned to Watson. His friend had suffered greatly because of Wicklow's actions, but now the truth had finally come to light.

Chapter 15

A week later, Dr Watson reclined in his armchair inside 221B Baker Street. A tartan blanket was draped across his legs despite his numerous protestations that he was perfectly capable of sitting without one. The bandage around his head had been reduced to a small square of gauze at his temple, covering the wound that had required several stitches.

Mrs Hudson entered with a laden tea tray, eyeing Watson with motherly concern.

"Another cup of tea, Doctor?" she asked, already pouring before he could answer. "And I've made those scones you're so fond of. You need building up after your ordeal."

"Mrs Hudson, I fear you'll have me resembling a prize pig at Smithfield Market if you continue at this rate," Watson said with a smile, though he accepted both tea and scone gratefully.

Holmes, who had been standing by the window watching the street below, turned to face the room. "Our good landlady has every right to fuss, Watson. You gave us quite a scare."

"It's been a week, Holmes. I am practically recovered."

"Practically is not the same as completely," Mrs Hudson chided, arranging the plates on the small table between the two armchairs. With a final satisfied nod, she retreated from the room.

Holmes took his seat opposite Watson, reaching for his pipe. "Lestrade sent word early this morning. They've concluded their investigation into Wicklow's affairs. It appears he was systematically poisoning several wealthy patients over the years, including Redford."

Watson shook his head slowly. "I still can't believe it. Wicklow was respected, admired even. To think he killed Redford all while I was treating the poor man, completely oblivious."

"The most effective deceptions often occur right before our eyes," Holmes said, lighting his pipe.

Watson stared into the fire. "What a waste of lives. Not just Redford, but Mrs Redford and Sarah who have been consumed with hatred for me."

"When I visited Sarah in prison a few days ago, she was devastated," Holmes said. "She wept when I told her about the evidence against Wicklow. She said she wished her mother could have known the truth before she died."

"Perhaps I should have looked into Redford's death more thoroughly," Watson said, the regret evident in his voice. "The symptoms were unusual, but not unheard of. I attributed them to a particularly virulent infection."

Holmes said, "You weren't to know, old friend. Wicklow deliberately administered the poison in small amounts to mimic natural illness. Even if you had suspected foul play, you had no reason to suspect him specifically."

"Still, I can't help but feel I could have done something. Has Sarah's case gone before the magistrate yet?" Watson asked.

"I'm not sure. I've asked Lestrade if the circumstances might be taken into account, but..." Holmes left the sentence unfinished, his expression suggesting little optimism.

"She pointed a gun at you, Holmes, and she kidnapped me."

"Yes. And the law must take its course. But one cannot help feeling that she too was a victim of Wicklow's callousness," Holmes replied. "Had he not poisoned her father and befriended her mother to cover his tracks, she might have led a very different life. Sarah told me that it was Wicklow who first planted seeds of doubt about you to her mother."

"The scoundrel!" Watson exclaimed.

Holmes said, "Don't let it upset you so. You are still recuperating."

They sat in contemplative silence for a minute or so.

Mrs Hudson appeared at the door again. "Inspector Lestrade is here to see you, Mr Holmes. Shall I send him up?"

Holmes and Watson exchanged a glance. "By all means, Mrs Hudson," Holmes replied.

Lestrade entered, removing his hat. "Afternoon, gentlemen. Dr Watson, good to see you on the mend."

"What brings you here, Inspector?" Holmes asked.

"Good news, for once," Lestrade said, remaining standing. "The Crown Prosecutor has reviewed Miss Redford's case. Given the extraordinary circumstances, they're considering a significantly reduced charge."

Watson's face lit up. "That is indeed good news."

Lestrade continued, "Dr Wicklow has made a full confession, not just to Redford's murder but to four others. He'll hang for his crimes, no doubt about that."

Holmes nodded solemnly. "Justice, though long delayed, is finally served."

"I'll be on my way," the inspector said. "Just wanted to let you know the good news."

After Lestrade had left, Holmes rose and moved to his violin case, removing the instrument with care. "Now, if you're truly on the mend, perhaps you'll indulge me in a little Bach? Mrs Hudson assures me it helps patients recover their strength."

"Far be it from me to contradict Mrs Hudson," Watson laughed, settling back in his chair.

As the first notes filled the room, Holmes observed his friend's peaceful expression with quiet satisfaction. He drew the bow across the strings with precision, reflecting on the events of Dr Redford's death. Even the most tangled webs of deception could not withstand the persistent pursuit of truth. He continued playing, content in the knowledge that order had been restored, justice served, and most importantly, that his friend was safe once more in the familiar confines of 221B Baker Street.

A note from the author

For as long as I can remember, I have loved reading mystery books. It started with Enid Blyton's Famous Five, and The Secret Seven. As I got older, I progressed to Agatha Christie books, and of course, Sir Arthur Conan Doyle's Sherlock Holmes.

I love the characters of Sherlock Holmes and Dr Watson, and the Victorian era that the stories are set in. It seemed only natural that one day, I would write some of my own Sherlock stories. I love creating new mysteries for Mr Holmes, and his trusty companion, Dr John Watson. It's not just the era itself that seems to ignite ideas within me; it's also the characters who were around at that time, and the lives they led.

This story has been checked for errors, but if you see anything we have missed and you'd like to let us know about them, please email mabel@mabelswift.com

You can hear about my new releases by signing up to my newsletter www.mabelswift.com As a thank you for subscribing, I will send you a free short story: Sherlock Holmes and The Curious Clock.

If you'd like to contact me, you can get in touch via mabel@mabelswift.com I'd be delighted to hear from you.

Best wishes

Mabel

Printed in Great Britain
by Amazon